THE EXECUTIVE SUITE

A THRILLER

LEAH ORR

"Very few of us are what we seem."

— Agatha Christie, *The Man in the Mist*

The Executive Suite

Leah Orr

First Edition: August 2021

ISBN: 979-8-5064-1221-2 paperback
ASIN: B0959QCP2C ebook
ISBN: 978-1-0879-6647-2 hardcover

Leah Orr
Jensen Beach, Florida
www.leahorr.com

Dedicated to all those who have been mistreated yet found the courage to right the wrongs of others for a better world and work environment.

Prologue

Anna called 911 at 9:54 p.m. on that thunder-clad evening. The young front desk intern spoke into her cell phone with an unsteady voice, traumatized by what she had just witnessed.

Anna had been printing out the evening's occupancy report when movement caught her peripheral vision. She jolted to her right, witnessing a flicker of light, blond hair, and flowing fabric mimicking a fallen angel in the moonlight. In a panic, Anna ran through the lobby to the rose garden in the courtyard. The body lay there, twisted and broken like a porcelain doll. Anna looked up and saw shadows pulling away from the executive suite's balcony. She recognized the fallen woman. From what she could tell, she looked like Janine, the general manager's secretary. Even in death, she was the most beautiful woman Anna had ever met.

When the police arrived at the Opulence Ocean Resort, the courtyard was filled with hotel guests trying to sneak a peek at the woman's lifeless body around the hotel security guards. The older cop spoke into his radio. He said the words "fatal" and "send transport." The younger cop was dry heaving into the pink azaleas.

Anna stood unresponsive, in shock, as she watched blood trickle, slowly flowing along the travertine tile. A river of crimson crept along the grout joints, pooling around the wishing well. She'd never seen so much blood in all her life.

Chapter One

The Executive Suite
Friday Evening

D rake, the assistant general manager, was the final team member to arrive. Making a dramatic entrance in true Drake style, he opened the door wide, demanding full attention. The others were nestled comfortably on the velvet sofa, rummaging through their cell phones, preoccupied with emails and finishing up last-minute business before the evening meeting would begin.

Drake apologized for being late as he sauntered across the foyer to the living area of the executive suite. Drake was impeccably dressed in a pale-blue Armani suit and a Georgia-peach-colored Ralph Lauren tie, which only he could pull off. He leaned back against the living room wall, adjusted his gold cuff links, and smiled brilliantly, as if he were modeling for *Esquire* magazine.

"Hello, everyone," Drake said calmly while silently contemplating why he and the others were summoned here on a Friday evening. Even stranger, why were they summoned to this suite? The twenty-fifth floor was not yet open to the public. Construction on this 7,000-square-foot executive suite—which donned exquisite designer furnishings, contemporary art, and state-of-the-art appliances—was not quite ready for paying guests.

The four-month renovation included cutting-edge security measures, such as soundproof and bulletproof windows, walls, and doors to safely accommodate political dignitaries, affluent business moguls, and Hollywood's rich and famous. *Condé Nast Traveler* magazine had recently released a piece about the Opulence's executive suite. The magazine called it "fit for a king" and "the perfect blend of lavish and sanctuary." To me, thought Drake, it's more bougie than lavish, more fit for a Kardashian than Prince Phillip, but nevertheless quite exquisite.

One of the executive suite's special features was a wood-paneled secret passage off the master bedroom leading to an elevator designed to bring guests down for a courtyard getaway, created to escape paparazzi and the fanfare of starstruck hotel guests.

Talia, the director of food and beverage, sat on the couch cross-legged, right foot shaking off nervous energy, and bore her usual resting bitch face. In spite of her beautiful, long black hair, cat-green eyes, and flawless skin, she was a bitch on wheels. In the male-dominated sales and catering profession, she had learned to create a tough exterior, so others were wise to tread lightly.

To her left sat Jason, the hotel's comptroller. He oversaw the hotel's entire financial operation. Jason was well-liked for his genius among top management, but to say he was a "strange bird" would be a grand understatement. Jason looked only at his hands and made little eye contact. He twitched his nose and blinked three times quickly, noticeably anxious about the meeting that was about to commence. Jason did not do well in groups. The hotel interns sometimes referred to him as "twitchy," and most people just thought he was a bit creepy. Jason was what most people would expect from someone who sits around crunching numbers all day in a dimly-lit, back-room cubicle. While most executive managers are rewarded with ocean-view offices, accounting is often considered the so-called redheaded stepchild of hotel management. Jason clearly ran one of the most important departments but carried very little respect.

Adam seemed rather comfortable all sprawled out on the Scandinavian-designed zero gravity recliner. He had recently been promoted from front desk manager to rooms director. He was good-looking in a Matthew McConaughey kind of way. Should anyone ask, he would be happy to entertain with his signature impression of the actor: "Alright, alright, alright!" Tall, fit, and tan, his smile melted all the old ladies' hearts. The blue-hairs smiled and giggled when they pranced by the front desk like teenage girls. Adam ran his fingers through his long surfer curls and winked at Talia but got no reaction.

Adam's cell phone dinged, then his smile dissipated. He stood up from the recliner, looking alarmed, when he noticed that his bank account was nearly wiped out of cash after the bank electronically paid his recent credit card bills. Feeling distraught, he put his phone in his pocket, trying to forget how financially leveraged to the hilt he was. His portfolio was diminishing daily, as many of his assets were worth far less now than when he first acquired them. Buying and selling properties at auction as a side hustle is not for the faint of heart. These days his only assets were a few choice stocks he bought early on. If it were not for Tesla and Bitcoin, he would be destitute.

Drake seemed startled when his cell phone unexpectedly vibrated. Aways the gentleman, with his salt-and-pepper hair and sophisticated good looks, he smiled and apologized for the interruption. He took out a pair of reading glasses from his inside jacket pocket to read the message on his phone, the way you would imagine 007 preparing for a mission. The teammates followed suit after a melodic string of sounds informed everyone of an incoming text message. The message came from Janine, the general manager's secretary. The message read:

Welcome to the Executive Suite. Let's get started.

Chapter Two

Janine

Our eyes don't lie; some say they are windows to the soul. They show us the truth, no matter what face we put on, no matter the situation. Just like our body language, our eyes give us away. The eyes will say more to you in an instant than any mix of over 170,000 words in the English language.

In truth, I knew I would take the job as executive secretary to Mr. Matheson within the first few minutes of our interview. His bright-blue eyes and Hugh Grant smile made me feel welcomed. A man with a kind soul, I thought.

"So tell me a bit about yourself," he asked with such sincerity that I imagine it could make some people uncomfortable. For me, his sincerity made me feel safe. I can attest to the fact that when a man makes a woman feel safe, an immediate bond of trust is created.

"I graduated cum laude from NYU's Tisch School of the Arts," I said proudly. "I write screenplays, and while I am actively sending my work to production houses, I write mostly in the evenings. Quite frankly, I need a full-time day job to help pay the bills and my student loans," I added.

"What brings you to Florida?" he asked inquisitively.

"I vacationed here for spring break last year. I stayed here in this hotel before and after our Caribbean cruise. I had such a great time that I knew, once I graduated, I wanted to live in Palm Beach."

"Tell me about why you would like to work in a hotel," he said.

"Working in a hotel seems a lot like being a character in a play," I suggested.

"How so?" he asked, seemingly intrigued by my observation.

"Well, every day new characters appear, and new adventures are created with every wedding or convention we entertain," I said.

"Tell me more. No one has ever compared the hotel industry to characters in a screenplay," he said.

"Okay, I'll set the scene for you," I explained. "You have your original cast, meaning all of your employees, then a convention checks in. Let's use the ballroom dance convention as an example.

"Over the course of the week, the Opulence Hotel transforms into a celebration of dance and music. In turn, everyone involved is affected by the new guests and the adventure begins. It is bewitching in a way; you can become enchanted with delight in the moment. It is very exciting.

"Then the ballroom dancers check out, a wedding celebration begins, and a brand new escapade ensues." I took a moment to collect my thoughts. "There never seems to be a dull moment, and there's a never-ending pool of characters to write about," I suggested. "I didn't mean to go off on a tangent, but I am very excited about the prospect of being a team member of such a delightful hotel in such an intriguing profession," I explained.

I was hired right there on the spot.

And so it begins.......

Chapter Three

The Executive Suite

J ust as the sun went down Friday evening, the doors in the executive suite locked with a thud and all the lights turned off. One moment they were enjoying the sunset through sixteen-foot, floor-to-ceiling windows; the next moment they were in total darkness.

Within a minute of Janine's text, they were locked in and shut off from the hotel's power grid. Small emergency lights turned on and barely illuminated the room.

"The power must have gone out," said Adam.

"Very observant," said Talia sarcastically.

Drake tried to open the executive suite's doors. "Locked," he said, disappointed. "Even if the electrician shut the power off, that does not explain why the doors are locked," he continued. "No one is expected to work on this floor over the weekend due to noise. We didn't want to create any problems with ToyCon, the toy convention checking in today."

"Someone check the secret passage off the master bedroom," suggested Adam.

"It's locked," yelled Talia from the master bedroom.

"How about the sliders to the terrace?" suggested Adam.

"Also locked," said Talia sadly.

"My cell phone has no service," cried Jason in a slight panic. "This is not good, this is not good, this is not good," Jason repeated over and over, annoying Talia.

"Enough, Twitchy!" shouted Talia, inadvertently calling Jason by his nickname. "Calm down; we can figure this out."

Just then, the TV flickered and turned on. A message on the screen read:

Admit what you have done, and get out alive.

Chapter Four

Janine

A great deal of effort goes into the first day of work. One cannot express the importance of making a good first impression. The initial impression is mostly made up of how you look, especially for a woman. Hair and makeup is just the beginning. Hair should look clean and stylish without looking too overdone—corporate chic if you will. Makeup should be fresh but slightly understated.

What to wear is a bigger challenge. Men barely struggle with what to wear to the office. A few different designer suits, white shirts, and an array of ties to switch off daily is all they need. Women, on the other hand, have it tougher. We want to be seen as feminine yet professional. Classy is not easy to pull off. A skirt cannot be too long or too short. A blouse cannot be too frilly or too sexy. I settled on a black Calvin Klein pantsuit, baby pink blouse, and Ferragamo heels.

I have to admit that getting all dressed up to start my first day was very exciting. It took me back to my Catholic school days with a perfectly pleated uniform and brand-new, shiny shoes.

"I am very excited to have you on our team," said Mr. Matheson sincerely. "You are going to love it here, but I must warn you that the hotel profession is tough," he explained. "Working for me, you will be held to the highest standard of professionalism, and you will be privy to very sensitive information. More importantly, you must be very discreet with the knowledge you attain." He paused for a moment, then sighed and smiled. "I cannot express this enough," he said emphatically.

"I understand," I said.

"I am confident you will make a great member of our team, Janine," he said reassuringly.

Chapter Five

The Executive Suite

The team members stared at the TV screen in shock. "What is this? Are we somehow stuck in a *Saw* movie?" said Talia sarcastically. "What's next? Are we going to have to somehow work together as a team, sacrifice a pound of flesh, and watch each of us die off one by one?" Talia laughed at the thought.

"That is a bit dramatic even for you, Talia," said Adam.

"This is ridiculous and not at all funny," declared Drake.

"What exactly is going on?" asked Adam. "I don't understand. This has got to be a joke. Maybe this is Mr. Matheson's idea of a team building exercise, you know, like an escape room. Maybe we should look around for clues."

Jason—sweating profusely at this point—said, "I knew it. I knew something like this could happen."

"What do you mean, you knew this could happen, Jason?" demanded Talia. "What is going on? Do you know something that we don't?"

"It's Janine. She knows everything that happens at the Opulence, and I'll bet this is some kind of twisted shakedown," Jason screeched, voice shaky with fear.

No one paid any attention to the grandfather clock in the living room chiming loudly eight times. The eighth chime unlocked a drawer at the bottom of the clock. An ear-piercing sound of a whistle filled the room as the drawer popped open. The drawer unveiled a green, old-fashioned hotel key with the number 617 etched in white.

Chapter Six

Janine

Mr. Matheson entered the executive conference room with the grace and dignity you would expect from a Kennedy or Hollywood royalty like Tom Hanks or George Clooney. A descendant of a prominent oil and gas tycoon, his position in society and financial circles, coupled with an Ivy League pedigree, served him very well.

"Hello, everyone. Say hello to Janine." Mr. Matheson winked at me from across the conference table in what was seemingly intended to be a gesture of encouragement. The team members turned my way and either nodded their heads or said hello.

"Janine is our new executive secretary and my personal assistant," said Mr. Matheson excitedly. "She will be your point person for weekly reports and the gatekeeper for all personal and professional executive hotel management business." Friendly eyes looked my way, and the staff seemed eager to welcome me to the team.

"From now on, any matters affecting the executive office will go through Janine," he stated.

The first thirty minutes on the job, meeting twenty-five executive managers at the Monday morning staff meeting, would make most people feel overwhelmed. I felt grand, with a sense of empowerment I had never quite felt before. In that moment, I was confident that Mr. Matheson and I would make a great team.

The staff were unaware that part of my role as executive secretary and personal assistant was to uncover theft and weed out abuse of power, and potentially corruption, in all areas of hotel management.

This is going to be great fun, I thought. I could almost see my future screenplay writing itself.

Chapter Seven

The Executive Suite

In every horror movie, there is that one pivotal moment where everyone knows they're fucked. This was that moment. The sheer look of horror on their faces, frozen in fear, when they stared at that key: priceless!

"What the hell is this?" Adam vented angrily. "What does this key mean?"

"Someone better start talking soon," threatened Talia.

Drake, the most senior manager in the group, picked up the key. He tried to calm everyone down. "Settle down. Let's try to figure this out rationally," he said assuringly. "Please, let's all sit down and talk this out."

Drake, Adam, and Talia walked back to the couch. Jason followed reluctantly.

"It is getting hot in here," Jason said in a cracking voice. He was starting to panic. He removed his jacket, took off his tie, and unbuttoned both of his shirt sleeves and rolled them up. Adam and

Drake did the same. Jason paced back and forth across the living room, and Talia removed her shoes.

"Seriously?" said Adam.

"Yes, seriously, dipshit," Talia snapped back. "I want to be comfortable too in this godforsaken lockbox."

Once Jason was settled and sat back down, Drake began to speak. "Okay, let's start at the beginning. How were we all summoned here?"

"I got a text from Janine about attending an important meeting in the executive suite at seven o'clock," said Talia.

"Me too," said Adam.

"Me too," said Jason.

"Same," said Drake. "Okay then, once we got here, the doors locked, the power went out, emergency lights turned on, and after a greeting welcoming us to the executive suite, the next message threatened us to admit what we have done to get out alive." Drake continued, "Then this green key was offered to us."

"What does this all mean?" asked Adam.

"No idea," said Jason.

Just then, the obnoxious whistle filled the room again, and a message appeared on the TV screen. It read:

John 8:32

"That's a Bible verse. I recognize it," said Talia. "Someone go and get the Bible from one of the nightstands in any one of the bedrooms."

"I'll go," said Adam. "Which one? The Book of Mormon or the Bible?"

"The Bible, you moron," quipped Talia.

"Here you go," said Adam, returning with the King James Bible.

Talia leafed through to John, chapter 8, verse 32. It read:

And ye shall know the truth, and the truth shall make you free.

"Here we go again with the truth message," said Adam. "Someone better talk soon. I refuse to be trapped in this place much longer."

Jason was visibly agitated. His shirt stuck to his skin from sweat, and he looked as though he was going to just melt into the couch. He blinked three times quickly, then stopped. He looked down at his pants: blink, blink, blink, stop, blink, blink, blink, stop. Wiping his hands on his pants from thigh to knee over and over, he shouted out, "It's me! The key belongs to me."

Chapter Eight

Janine

My first week at work was long and arduous. Just trying to wrap my brain around the collection and analysis of all the daily reports was hard enough, but dealing with unhappy guests is something else.

I have encountered some of the most intriguing people in some of the most unusual circumstances. The general manager's office is the place a guest winds up when other managers don't resolve their problems well enough.

Mrs. Cunningham, for example, came to visit, complaining that the hot water in her room was not hot enough, while Mr. Katz, who stayed in that same room last week, complained that the water was too hot. *Scalding* was the word he used.

Ms. Wallace apologized for her ninety-year-old husband defecating in the bed. She said she tried to clean it, but it was hopeless. She offered to pay for the damages, which of course we did not accept. "Accidents happen," I said in my most empathetic voice.

Mr. Madison complained about a woman lying on the beach topless. I saw her as well. I can't imagine anyone would complain about that. She was beautiful. He said the woman made his wife feel uncomfortable. That I can understand. I've seen his wife. Let's just say, she's quite robust!

The most disturbing visit was from a young woman named Susan. She stayed with us frequently between flights. She was a pilot, and her crew enjoyed a beach stay whenever they landed in West Palm Beach.

"There was a man staring at me through the garden terrace while I was on the phone," she explained. "At first I didn't think anything of it, but after my shower, I saw him again. He had his face pressed up against the glass sliding door, seemingly trying to sneak a peek when I was wrapped in a bath towel."

I was aghast and did not really know what to say. "I'll call Tim in security," I said. Tim helped her fill out an incident report. "Would you like for me to call the police?" offered Tim.

"No," said Susan. "That is not necessary."

After the report was filled out, Susan asked if she could speak with me alone. "Of course," I said. I locked the office door, momentarily keeping out any visitors, and then sat back down.

Susan said timidly, "I think I know who this creeper peeper is."

"Tell me," I said firmly.

"I pointed him out this morning to the front desk clerk; she said his name is Jason. I think he works in accounting."

Chapter Nine

The Executive Suite

Like a cemetery on a winter evening, silence filled the room. No one stirred, moved, or made any sound at all. They just glared at Jason, waiting for an explanation. Jason rarely raised his voice. He never even spoke in a staff meeting unless he was asked a specific question. Even then, he would answer softly with a precise but brief statement. So when Jason cried out, "It's me! The key belongs to me," they were ready to listen.

The team members waited impatiently for Jason to collect his thoughts, eyes fixated on him.

"Okay," he said. Remarkably, he seemed to be in control of his blinking twitch. Suddenly calmer, hands folded on his lap, he straightened his back and raised his head to meet the eyes of his colleagues. He began telling his story. "When I was working at the Miami

Airport Hotel, I saved a woman's life."
He paused, took a deep breath, and
continued. "I saw a man hit her through
the terrace window," he said. "I grabbed
a room key from the front desk, and I
saved her."

"What do you mean, you 'saved her'?
How?" asked Drake inquisitively.

"I opened the door, took the knife
from my pocket, and stabbed him," said
Jason coldly. "He's dead."

"Oh. My. God," said Talia, seemingly
shocked by his emotionless portrayal of
the story. Suddenly Jason didn't seem
so twitchy anymore, thought Talia. She
wondered if her colleagues noticed that
his mannerisms had changed. He
suddenly appeared very calm and
calculating, his eyes—cold and lifeless
—staring directly at her.

At that moment, a voice came over
the suite's speaker system:

"That's not the whole story, is it?"

"I know that voice," said Adam. "It's
Janine."

The whistle again! That piercing
whistle! Everyone covered their ears.

Then a box dropped from the air vent sixteen feet above. As the vent clamored shut, the teammates looked stunned. The box dropped directly onto the exquisite, jade marble Nella Vetrina coffee table.

"Open it," demanded Adam.

Jason reached for the box, but Drake grabbed hold of it first. "I'll open it," said Drake, trying to take control of the situation. "Give me your knife, Jason. I assume you still keep a knife in your pocket?" Old habits die hard, he thought.

Jason could feel the weight of Drake's stare and intention and reluctantly handed over the folding Kershaw serrated pocketknife with a three-inch blade.

"I'll keep this," said Drake as he forcefully grabbed the knife from Jason's hand.

Drake sliced through the duct tape and opened the box. Inside was an issue of the *Miami Herald* dated May 2, 1989. The headline read:

Hero or Peeping Tom?

A Miami man, Cal Jones, was found dead in a Miami Airport Hotel room at 11:30 p.m. Monday. His girlfriend, flight attendant Alicia Wilson, said hotel accountant, Jason McNeil, fearing she was in danger, unlocked her hotel room and killed her boyfriend. Police are investigating whether or not Ms. Wilson was in danger at the time, and if so, how Mr. McNeil was aware of the incident.

"So let me get this straight," said Talia. "You saw a woman in danger, grabbed a key from the front desk, opened her door, and stabbed her boyfriend with your knife. Is that correct?"

"Stabbed and killed," added Adam.

"I have so many questions," Talia continued. "Why were you looking in her room? Why didn't you call security? Why do you carry a hunting knife to work? Did you know this girl? Was she actually in danger? Were you just jealous she had another man in her room? How did you see her being hit if she was in room 617? Wasn't that on the sixth floor?"

Jason threw both hands up above his head. "Hold up," he said, trying to get Talia to slow down. "Well, first of all, the Miami Airport Hotel is a one-story hotel," explained Jason. "The 617 room was the Boston room: Red Sox, Celtics, Bruins themed. All the rooms were big-city themed, and room numbers were the area codes. You know, like 202 Washington DC, 212 New York City, 303 Denver, et cetera. Whatever the area codes were back in 1989. The themed rooms made travelers feel at home when they spent most of their time away from it." Jason paused then continued, "My hunting knife is for saf—" Jason was interrupted.

"Hold up," said Drake, raising his right hand, motioning him to stop. "There is something else in the box: an incident report."

"What incident report?" asked Jason, perplexed and visibly upset.

"It's an incident report from about a month ago," explained Drake. "The report is about a woman named Susan, no last name." That's weird, thought Drake.

"It says here that she is a pilot and stays here at the Opulence often," Drake went on. "She said that a man had been watching her through the sliding glass door on her first-floor garden terrace. She also said that this was not the first time and that she thinks that the perpetrator was Jason in accounting."

"Well, Jason, you definitely have a thing for women and planes," Talia said sarcastically.

"My mother was a flight attendant," explained Jason. "She died when I was young. I loved her. Sometimes women remind me of her, and I just want to get to know them and protect them," he said unconvincingly.

"Or stalk and kill them," said Adam, seemingly trying to anger Jason.

"I didn't kill that man on purpose. I thought he was hurting her," said Jason.

"Thought?" said Talia angrily. "Thought?"

"When I saw that man choking my sweet Alicia, I thought she was in danger, so I broke in and killed him," he admitted.

"'My sweet Alicia'? You knew her?" asked Talia. "Originally you said he hit her. Now you say he was choking her. Which is it?"

"Yes, I knew her," said Jason calmly. "We were friends. I wanted more, but she had a boyfriend who mistreated her. Turns out, according to the police, she liked to be smacked around," he explained. "Role-playing, I think, is what some people call it. I don't remember now if he was hitting her or choking her. He was hurting her."

"So you actually killed someone for no good reason," said Adam accusingly.

"He was an asshole who was going to kill her eventually. I just know it," said Jason assuringly.

"And this woman in our hotel? Is she in danger?" asked Adam. "We keep all airline staff on the first floor with a garden atrium view. Should we be worried about other women?"

"No!" Jason was very angry now. He yelled up to the speaker in the ceiling, "Well, now you know my secret! LET ME OUT OF HERE!"

Chapter Ten

Janine

When I told Mr. Matheson about the incident report and the implication that Jason could be a peeping tom, he seemed unsurprised.

"Do me a favor and call around to a few places he worked before landing a job here," he suggested. "Something always seemed a bit off to me about that guy; I would like to learn more about him."

"Well, if this guy turns out to be a creeper, shouldn't you fire him?" I asked.

"I am going to tell you something that may upset you, but you are in the real world now. This is not college." He sounded fatherly in that moment, like he really cared and sincerely wanted me to understand. I was intrigued, waiting with bated breath for what he was going to say next.

"Here is the thing you need to learn about corporate America and this company: when you are excellent at your job, there is almost NOTHING you can do to get fired. The company has your back. If there is a problem in your hotel, they'll move you to another. The good news for an excellent manager? The company has your back. The bad news about an excellent manager? The company has your back."

"Well, that is disturbing," I said, shocked.

"So, just like priests in the Catholic Church getting caught abusing the parishioners' children, they get moved to a different parish?"

"Yup, just like that," he said sadly. "There are hundreds of thousands of instances of pastoral abuse worldwide; now ask me how many priests still have a job?"

"How many?" I asked.

"All of them!"

Chapter Eleven

The Executive Suite

The three-hundred-year-old grandfather clock, donated to the hotel from a descendant of the McGregor family in Scotland, chimed nine times.

"Holy crap, it's nine o'clock already," said Talia. "I can't believe we have been trapped here for two hours already. I am starving. Let's see what there is to eat and drink in this place."

"Housekeeping was supposed to get the suite ready for guests' arrival. We were hoping to entertain our first guests as early as next week," said Adam. "Let's see if they stocked the refrigerator and minibar."

The teammates nearly knocked each other over fighting to get to the kitchen first. There were twelve Fiji water bottles in the Sub-Zero refrigerator.

"We have water," said Talia excitedly. She handed the water bottles to all of her colleagues.

On the granite counter was a large, wicker welcome basket full of Florida oranges, Clif Bars, and Sunchips. Talia handed out snacks to everyone as well. "Nothing in the minibar," she said, obviously disappointed.

"Well, we might as well get more comfortable. No telling how much longer we will be here," said Drake with a sigh.

"Don't be so casual about this, Drake," said Talia. "This is not the Big Brother House. We are not supposed to hang out and have fun until we get voted out. We've been kidnapped."

Adam laughed loudly, and Jason squirmed.

"You know what I think?" suggested Talia.

"Tell me, Talia. I can't wait to hear this," said Drake dismissively.

"I think this is an exit interview."

"What makes you say that?" said Drake.

"I can answer that best, I think," said Adam. "I was thinking the same thing. I was very involved in the renovation of this suite. We set up a speaker system, video surveillance, and sound system for security so that dignitaries and high-profile guests do not have to be with their hired security staff 24/7. Their security team could be in the guest suite next door and just watch and listen in without infringing upon their privacy."

Suddenly all eyes were on Adam. He'd caught the attention of every teammate. "If you look closely at the ceiling, you can see all of the hardware installed. Cameras and microphones are in every room except the bathroom and bedrooms."

"Where exactly are you going with this?" asked Drake.

"My guess is that Janine is taping and listening to everything going on in here, and if any one of us confesses to something or does something rash, then she can take it to human resources and we would be terminated."

"I need to sit down," said Talia, suddenly feeling a bit woozy.

"Me too," said Jason.

"Don't sit near me, Jason Voorhees," said Adam, trying to be witty.

"He's more of a Norman Bates than a Jason Voorhees," said Talia with a giggle. "You know, a little less *Friday the 13th* and more *Psycho* creeper hotelier with mommy issues, to be a bit more accurate."

"Very funny, Talia and Adam," mused Jason. "Don't think I don't know what you have been up to at the front desk, Adam. As the comptroller, I put together all the financial reports. It's funny, ever since you started managing the desk, very little cash is collected; I wonder where all that cash goes."

Then, suddenly—silence.

Within five minutes they were all asleep. A little GHB in the water had knocked them all out.

Dream on, my fair teammates. An exit interview and severance pay is the least of your worries.

Chapter Twelve

Janine

Another day and more guest visitors, a few incident reports from the manager on duty, and lots of daily reports from the front desk, food and beverage, and accounting. I think it is utterly unnecessary just how many reports are compiled in nearly every department every day. Most are redundant. Someone needs to figure out a better way to streamline all of these reports into just one, and don't get me started about the waste of paper and the killing of trees.

The old lady in room 2022 complained that she could hear the "Ahem,"—she cleared her throat and whispered—"men in the room next door doing unspeakable things to each other." I could not help but smile a little. Ugh, old people, I thought.

The housekeeping department filled out an incident report about a four-foot king snake that was left behind in a bathtub. Thank God for Barry in engineering; he is not afraid of anything. He easily removed it and found a new home for it in the garden of the hotel next door. A gift from a friendly neighbor seemed fair in my mind. They often refuse to let us use their extra parking lot for overflow even when they are not at all busy.

Mr. Matheson returned from lunch on a tear, evidently very angry. "Janine, can you get me the daily rooms' reports from the front desk for the last few weeks?" he asked. "Both arrivals and departures reports, please."

"Sure, I'd be happy to," I said. After pulling the reports and taking a bit of time to read through them, I noticed that most nights there were three or four rooms closed out for maintenance issues. Yet I did not notice these rooms on the list for maintenance to fix or any work order requests crossing my desk for approval. That's suspicious, I thought.

When I told Mr. Matheson my concern, he asked me to look into it. He told me to pull the room keys and go to each room to see if anything was broken. Then he asked me to visit maintenance and ask to see the work log to determine if anyone had entered those rooms on those evenings. Then he asked me to report back to him.

I found that the rooms were in perfect order, everything in its appropriate place, and maintenance was not called to any of those rooms for repairs. Very peculiar, I thought.

I spoke with Anna—one of our youngest interns, who just graduated from the University of Miami—about rooms being blocked nightly for maintenance.

Anna said, "I don't want to get anyone in trouble, but once, I saw a lady check in who wanted to pay in cash. Adam took the money to the back room instead of the register, and I saw him put the money in his pocket. Then he blocked the room on the computer and put "maintenance" in the notes section. Please don't tell anyone. I like my job. I want to keep it."

Housekeeping later confirmed that they were often asked to clean rooms that were not on their daily room occupancy list. And just like that, if there

is something you want to know, just ask
the front desk clerks. They know
everything.

Chapter Thirteen

The Executive Suite
Saturday Morning

The sunrise on the coast of Palm Beach is stunning. Cascading colors of yellow and orange dance around in delight and rejuvenate the soul. This is one of the many reasons a thousand people move to Florida every day.

While the hotel guests enjoyed the spectacle in the sky, equally mesmerized by the rolling waves in the sea, the teammates were slowly waking from their slumber.

The grandfather clock clanged seven times.

Talia woke up first. "What time is it?" she shouted. "Oh no, we all fell asleep!"

"I don't feel so good," said Adam.

"I feel like we were drugged," said Drake.

"Where is Jason?" asked Adam.

"Look around. Now," demanded Talia.

"You are so damn bossy!" said Adam.

After a few minutes of searching through the executive suite, Drake said, "He's gone. Either he escaped or she let him go."

"She said she would if we told the truth," said Adam. "Oh no, it is seven o'clock on Saturday. My goldfish! I need to get out of here to feed my goldfish."

"We are prisoners of some whack-ass secretary in a demented game of *Tell Me Your Secrets* like it's a new board game from Mattel, and you are worried about your stupid goldfish," complained Talia. "Just shoot me now and get this over with! My God!"

"My mouth is dry like cotton balls, and I've got a splitting headache," said Drake. "And . . . well, we obviously can't drink the water."

The TV flickered and turned on. An image appeared: a photograph of Jason in handcuffs in the back of a police cruiser.

"Serves him right," said Adam. "He was a freaking psychopath . . . or sociopath, whichever."

"Holy shit," said Talia excitedly. "Janine is one badass bitch."

Chapter Fourteen

Janine

No one ever achieves great success alone. Successful people can pinpoint a person or two who realized a certain potential— a potential that maybe they had not yet seen in themselves. A person who took them under their wing, taught them everything they knew, and prepared them for the very bright future they aspired to achieve. That is what they call a mentor.

Mr. Matheson was my mentor: general manager of the Opulence Hotel in Palm Beach by the age of thirty-eight. The hotel was a beacon of beauty and elegance in the hotel industry. The 1,200 rooms on this forty-acre beachfront property made it even more appealing for large, multimillion-dollar corporate conventions. Companies fought for popular dates to unwind by our sandy shores, and brides bickered about having to set their wedding dates two years in advance in order to book the famous Grand Diamond Ballroom.

Mr. Matheson was kind, impeccably professional in every way, and just brilliant. He was a step ahead of everyone. When I offered discrepancies on the daily reports, he had already found the errors. When I suggested ways to handle an unhappy guest, he would finish my sentences as if we were sharing the same thought. Most importantly, when I had to report back to him about an executive manager's indiscretions, he already knew about them. He had an uncanny way of just knowing things, like he could look right into your eyes and read your soul—a true gift.

Chapter Fifteen

The Executive Suite

That damn whistle again. Cold air gusted through the air vents above, and crisp, green dollar bills fell like rain, about a hundred of them. The grandfather clock chimed nine times, and the song "Mo Money Mo Problems" by The Notorious B.I.G. played from the executive suite's speakers.

♫ *"I don't know what they want from me*
It's like the more money we come across
The more problems we see" ♫

While the teammates were distracted by this grand spectacle, a door slammed in the master bedroom. Everyone rushed into the bedroom. On the bed was a carefully placed, large manila envelope with Adam's name written on it.

"Your turn," said Talia.

"Janine must have come in by the hidden passage," said Adam.

"Why wouldn't she just leave it here when we were asleep or drop it from the vent?" asked Drake.

"Because Janine is all about theatrics," explained Talia. "She was a theatre or drama major or . . . screenplay . . . songwriter, who knows, some shit like that at NYU. I'll bet she wanted to first rain on us with money, accompany that with a soundtrack, then offer the envelope. You know, suspense, intrigue, and mystery. Don't you two know anything about women? Don't answer that."

"Well, are you going to open it? Or should I?" asked Drake.

"I'll do it," said Adam with a sigh.

"Actually, I'll read it out loud to the group," demanded Drake. He snatched the envelope quickly from the bed before Adam had the chance. Inside was a handwritten note.

I know how much money you stole from the hotel. The amount is nearly $75,000 over the past 18 months. I will keep your secret. You will visit human resources and quit on Monday. But before you do that, you will sign over your Tesla stock to me. The documents are enclosed for your signature. I will sell the stock and repay the hotel what you stole. You will also sign over your Bitcoin. I will cash that in for myself. Consider that your penance, and be happy I will not turn you in to the police.

"You stole money from the hotel?" asked Drake. "Yeah, now I remember something that Jason said right before we passed out from the drugs in our water. He said cash was disappearing from the front desk."

"I am not going to answer that," said Adam. "She wants us to admit crimes. At least the bedrooms are not wired for sound or video."

"So you think someone took the time to plan and trap the four of us but not wire all the rooms for sound or video? Sometimes I wonder, Adam, what is going on between those ears of yours," said Talia. "Your logic is exhausting."

"I am not signing this," said Adam. "This is bullshit."

"From where I'm standing, you have two choices: go to jail for felony theft or pay the bitch. I'd go for the latter," Talia said with a grin.

Adam took the paperwork and a pen, walked into the office connected to the master bedroom, and slammed the French doors.

"He better think long and hard about signing those papers," said Talia. "Blackmail is a nice touch. I love it. I doubt she will *actually* take any money for herself, but I love it!"

"Now what?" said Drake. "He signs the papers, then what? How do we get out of here? What is in store for us?"

"I don't freaking know. What did *you* do, Drake?" asked Talia. "What sinister tale do *you* have to tell? What God-awful circumstance put you here in this suite?"

"I could ask the same about you, Talia. What sinister tale do *you* have to tell?

Silence ensued between the two, and a staredown continued until Drake finally broke down and asked, "What is taking Adam so long? He has been in there for a while now."

Suddenly they heard a series of thuds and then a door slamming shut.

Panic-stricken, Drake said, "What in the hell was that?"

"I'll go check on him," said Talia, running into the office. "Shit! He's gone."

"What do you mean, 'he's gone'?" asked Drake rhetorically.

"He disappeared, Drake. Just like Jason."

Chapter Sixteen

Janine

There is a powerful connection between a dad and his daughter: a bond that is unbreakable, a love unconditional.

I have great memories of my dad dancing with my sister and me at father-daughter dances at our parish. Memories of playing in the pool on Sunday afternoons and him throwing us up in his arms and the sound of childhood giggles fill my head.

One Friday, a beautiful young woman walked into the office asking to speak with her dad. I said, "Your dad? I'm sorry, who is your dad?"

"My dad is Mr. Matheson," she said.

"Oh, I am so sorry. I am new here," I admitted. "I didn't know Mr. Matheson was married. I did not know he had children."

"Just me," she said. "Mom is dead. She died here at the hotel. You should ask him to tell you about it sometime."

Speechless, I took a moment to absorb the shock of her statement. I finally replied, "Oh my, I am so sorry." My heart sank deep into my chest as I saw the pained expression on her face. That is so very sad, I thought.

Suddenly so many thoughts filled my mind. How did I not know this? Why didn't anyone tell me this? I wondered why he had no family photos on his desk, but I thought it was because he was unmarried. I felt incompetent. I had been working here for two months at this point, and I should have known about this. Mr. Matheson is always so concerned about my well-being and how *I* am enjoying my job, but *I* never asked how *he* is doing. I felt so selfish. He must be in pain every day knowing that his wife died in the very place he works.

I snapped my thoughts back. "He has been away from the hotel for the past few days, but I expect him back later this afternoon. He is in Miami attending the Seatrade Cruise Global convention with a few of our sales managers," I explained.

"What is that?" the woman asked.

"Every September the cruise ship industry meets at the convention center in Miami to showcase the latest technology in the cruise industry and build stronger relationships with upscale hotels to partner with. Many cruise passengers extend their vacation on the front or back end of their voyage with a hotel stay. We are trying to get a larger share of that business since our hotel is located close enough to both Port Everglades in Fort Lauderdale and Port Canaveral in Orlando."

"Oh, sounds fun," she said. "My name is Gracie." She extended her hand to shake mine. I shook her hand and immediately felt her self-confidence.

Just then, Drake walked into the office. "Hey, Gracie," he said excitedly. "How is school? We sure do miss you around here. The days are just not the same without your beautiful, smiling face greeting us every morning."

"I am great, Drake. School is going well, and I miss you too," she said warmly.

He gave her a big bear hug, lingering a few moments longer than a typical greeting, in my opinion. He said, "It is so good to see you. Make sure you visit your mom's grave while you are in town, I am sure she would love for you to bring her flowers." Then Drake continued on into his office.

Perplexed, I said, "You two know each other well!"

"Yes," said Gracie. "Drake has worked with my dad for twenty years or so. He is also a close family friend, almost like a second dad to me," she explained. "Anyway, I drove all the way from school to surprise my dad, but since he is not here right now, would you like to go to lunch?" she asked. "Maybe by the time we get back he will be back in the office."

"I'd love to," I said excitedly.

Chapter Seventeen

The Executive Suite

Drake and Talia stared at the bookcase against the wood-paneled wall of the office. Five books had been displaced from the top shelf and strewn across the hardwood floor. An access control keypad was revealed in the top corner of the shelf.

"This is not just a bookcase, Talia. It's also a punch-coded access door."

"No shit, Sherlock," quipped Talia. "You really are captain obvious."

Drake did not seem at all annoyed by Talia's sarcasm. He was the consummate professional at all times. "I'll bet Adam knew about this door and the passcode along with it. Remember, he helped design this suite. Why didn't he tell us about this door yesterday? We all could have gotten out of here. Even if he forgot about it until now, why lock the door behind him? Why would he leave us here?"

"You are the assistant general manager. Why do you know so little about this suite?" asked Talia. "You and Mr. Matheson walk around this hotel for hours every day, checking every nook and cranny, but you expect me to believe you know nothing about this suite?"

"Mr. Matheson and I have worked together for the past twenty years. We are friends, like family even. We trust each other completely, but we work separately. He has me involved in mostly back-of-the-house stuff, like housekeeping, the kitchen, maintenance, and the loading dock. He oversees the staff and front of the house, like the front desk, dining room, lobby bar, and catering and sales departments," explained Drake. "This is actually the first time I have been in this suite."

They now focused on the Macassar ebony and leather desk designed by Taylor Llorente. Drake said, "Look. He left the papers behind—unsigned."

Chapter Eighteen

Janine

Gracie and I had a lovely lunch outdoors at Renato's. I love Italian food. In my opinion, Renato's is one of the best Italian restaurants in Palm Beach. Authentic Italian cuisine is hard to find. We shared the melanzane alla parmigiana, which is roasted Sicilian eggplant with bufala mozzarella cheese, and gnocchi con burrata, which is gnocchi with burrata cheese imported from Italy. I have such fond memories of my mother making gnocchi from scratch. These days, I get back home to Connecticut just a few times a year, so Renato's is as close as I can get to the warm feelings of home.

It was a beautiful afternoon. Melodies of birds in the distance, soft Italian music, and a lovely table on the terrace —set with the traditional white tablecloth and red-and-white-checkered napkins— along with seventy-five-degree weather made for a perfect day to enjoy lunch outdoors. After Gracie's fake Florida ID passed scrutiny with the waitress, we ordered a bottle of pinot grigio. I snatched her ID from her when the waitress disappeared into the kitchen. "Nice ID," I said. "Looks legit."

"It's real. I have a friend who works at the DMV, and he may have typed my birth year incorrectly," she said with a girlish giggle. "Don't tell my dad."

"Your secret is safe with me," I assured her. This girl is a real rebel, I thought, and right away I felt like I had known Gracie all my life.

Just like me, she was a great lover of the arts. She was a theatre studies major, studying at the University of Central Florida. But she, unlike me, was interested in theatre design and technology. She was honing her skills in costume design, stagecraft, sound, lighting, and special effects.

"We would make a great team," I suggested. "I could write screenplays, and you could bring them to life. Just imagine, Cannes film festival 2026. That would give us plenty of time to create something spectacular."

"Sounds great, but I'm struggling right now just trying to get through my script analysis class," said Gracie.

"I would be happy to help you with that class," I said enthusiastically. "Script writing and analysis is my specialty."

We hadn't been back from lunch for ten minutes before Mr. Matheson returned from the Seatrade convention in Miami.

"I see you two have met," said Mr. Matheson happily. "Wow, seeing you side by side, you two look like twins. I knew there was something I really liked about you, Janine."

Chapter Nineteen

The Executive Suite

That loud, shrill, high-pitched sound filled the suite once again.

The whistle, so horrible, made Drake and Talia's faces contort, as if they were enduring crippling pain.

Back in the living room, the TV flickered and turned on. It was a video this time.

On the screen were two police officers: a very young, thin officer who couldn't be more than twenty-five years old and a portly, older cop. They stopped Adam in the hotel's courtyard. The younger officer took out a small card from his pants pocket. He read Adam his Miranda rights as the older cop took his hands behind his back, one after the other, and handcuffed him. Adam said nothing as he was whisked away.

The video stopped, and the TV turned off.

A few moments of silence ensued. Then, over the speakers in the executive suite, they heard these words of warning:

"Adam made the wrong choice. Will you?"

Chapter Twenty

Janine

A week passed before I could gather up enough courage to ask Mr. Matheson about his wife.

"If you don't mind me asking, Mr. Matheson, what exactly happened to your wife?"

"I am assuming Gracie mentioned my wife's death to you over lunch?" he asked. "I knew you would ask me soon enough." He asked me to close the door behind me and take a seat.

"She fell to her death off an eighth-floor balcony," he said sadly. "It happened about a year ago. It pains me to say that I believe she was having an affair with one of our executive managers. They would allegedly meet in a suite periodically, right here in this hotel, right under my nose. If true, I am not sure that I will ever get over that."

"I am so sorry," I said sincerely.

"Suite 820 has been locked and off-limits for use ever since the incident. I know that her supposed lover was one of our executive managers because video surveillance of that floor and the elevator have been wiped clean during that time period," he explained. "Only an executive manager would have access to that footage."

"What did the police say?" I asked. "Do they think it was foul play or an accident?"

"The investigation is ongoing," he said. "In fact, since the incident, we have had two Palm Beach detectives check in on us routinely as they continue to gather evidence, but whenever I ask about the case, they blow me off and offer little information. The detectives just appease me by saying, 'We're on it, Mr. Matheson. We're on it!'"

Chapter Twenty-One

The Executive Suite

And then there were two. The grandfather clock chimed twelve times.

"It's noon, and we have been here since yesterday evening with only tainted water and a few crappy snacks left," said Talia, frustrated. "It has been quite some time since we heard from Janine. Let's get this over with. Tell me what you did."

"No, you tell me what you did," Drake shot back. A few minutes of silence followed. The only noise was the ticktock of the grandfather clock.

"So, Drake, we are just going to sit here and stare at each other until one of us gives in from starvation or exhaustion or Janine forces our hand? Is that how this is going to go?"

"I guess so," said Drake unapologetically. He got up from the living room couch, trudged into the kitchen, grabbed an orange, and lobbed it over to Talia. He took an orange for himself and returned to the couch. Talia sat down on the leather recliner across from the couch, leaning back, making herself comfortable. They watched each other peel their oranges. Talia demonstrated a perfect peel, one long string of skin. Drake, on the other hand, picked off small bits of skin, collected the rinds, and placed them on the coffee table, one on top of the other, creating a precarious tower.

"Hey, that coffee table is worth thousands of dollars. Have a little respect," said Talia, expecting more from a hotel assistant general manager. "Collect your mess and dispose of it properly." Ugh, men are such pigs, she thought.

After a proper disposal of the rinds, an air of mistrust filled the room, as if you could cut through it with a knife. It was palpable, even to watch. They ate their oranges in silence, never taking their eyes off of each other.

Chapter Twenty-Two

Janine

Gracie visited her dad for the weekend from time to time, and we would often have lunch on Friday afternoons. Because Mr. Matheson knew we had become fast friends and our luncheons would often consist of a few cocktails, he usually gave me the remainder of the day off.

Gracie would tell me all about her classes at school and college parties and show me pictures of some pretty fantastic set designs she created for plays at school. The set design for *Dracula* was jaw-dropping. It was so hard to believe college students could create such a masterpiece. The backdrop of Castle Dracula, otherwise known as Bran Castle, in Transylvania was astounding. I had no doubt that this stage would most definitely be in contention for the scenic design award at the Southeastern Theatre Conference (SETC) this year.

"Were you always into set design or did you use to act as well?" I asked.

"In middle and high school I used to act. My favorite was the role of Peter Pan. In that play I got to fly with the use of the theatrical fly system, which is a series of cables, pulleys, and counterweights. It was then that I became enamored with the mechanics behind the scenes that brought the whole play together. You know, where the magic is made."

Gracie told stories such as: high school backdrops falling on the performers, wigs falling off the actors, and one time when the entire set was stolen before opening night as a senior prank.

In return, I would entertain Gracie with elaborate stories about hotel guests and their strange complaints, and we would laugh for hours. I also intrigued her with some of the screenplays I wrote in college, mostly horror stories and thrillers. I love haunted houses and hotels. I told her that one day I would like to write a screenplay about a haunted hotel.

"Wouldn't it be great if you wrote a screenplay about one of Florida's famous haunted hotels like the La Concha hotel in Key West?" Gracie suggested. "You know the one; that's the hotel with the ghost that jumps off the roof every night."

"What? I've never heard of that hotel before," I said. "Tell me more."

"Well, the La Concha hotel was built in 1926 on Duvall Street. At six stories tall, it is the tallest building in Key West. Be wary of ordering a glass of chardonnay because the rumor is that, on the rooftop bar where the spa is now, at least thirteen people have jumped off, committing suicide. One man was drinking chardonnay before leaping to his death, and apparently his ghost can still be seen falling from the roof today. Another man died when he fell down the elevator shaft in the 1980s."

"We should visit one day," I said in delight. "How fun."

I was surprised, however, that Gracie chose that haunted hotel in particular. I thought she would be somewhat sensitive to the idea of people falling or jumping to their death, knowing the peculiar circumstances of her own mother's demise. She speaks of her mother's death with such callousness and disdain that I wonder if she truly ever grieved for her or if she is still just very angry about her mother's alleged affair.

Aside from the strange haunted hotel suggestion, she and I were alike in many ways. Not only did we look alike—same hair color and body shape, which was tall and thin—we also shared a similar major in college and both had a love for the art of storytelling. With my love of script and her love of set design, we would often imagine, just for fun, what would transpire if we mixed certain plays or musicals together. What if Dr. Frankenstein's monster happened upon the junkyard in *Cats*, the musical? What if the tornado from Oz brought Dorothy to the demon barber of Fleet Street in *Sweeney Todd*?

One time our waitress, chuckling at one of our silly scenarios, stated, "You two are trouble."

She got that right!

Chapter Twenty-Three

The Executive Suite

Two hours passed, and neither Drake nor Talia uttered a word to each other. The grandfather clock clanged two times. It was Saturday afternoon, and at this point they were uncomfortably hot, hungry, and exhausted. Feeling physically tired and mentally defeated, they both drifted off to sleep for about two hours.

Drake was the first to wake. He began roaming around the suite, touching every conceivable crinkle in the wallpaper and wood paneling, hoping against all hope that he would find a crevice where another secret door would be revealed. He looked under area rugs, lifted vases, sifted through books, opened the kitchen cabinets, and finally confronted the grandfather clock, asking it, "Do you have any other secrets to tell?"

When Talia awoke, she walked to the bathroom in the master bedroom. "With no running water, you can't even flush the toilets in this shithole." She swore at the commode, uttered other words no one should ever hear, then slammed the lid.

Drake greeted Talia with a board game in his hands when she returned to the living room.

"What is that?" said Talia.

"It's Scrabble."

"I don't want to play."

"Come on, there is nothing else to do here until Janine lets us out. Let's play," begged Drake.

"Okay, I give in," said Talia.

They sat at the opal-colored Bernhardt dining table with black-and-dark-gray paisley upholstered chairs—understated for the room but practical for the hotel. Dark, busy fabrics hide the mess or spills guests leave behind. For a hotel that boasts 85–95 percent occupancy year-round, fabric choice is essential.

"How many tiles do you start with?" asked Drake.

"Seven," answered Talia. "Whomever has the word with the most letters will start. The game is more interesting that way. It provides more choices for the other player."

"Then I'll go first," said Drake. "I have a seven-letter word: *riptide.* First word on the board is a double word score. That's twenty points."

Using the *D* from *RIPTIDE*, Talia put down the remaining letters to spell D-R-U-G-G-E-D. "That's seventeen points, triple letter score for the *U* and the *D*. *Drugged,* just like we were drugged yesterday."

"Very funny, Talia. Your sense of humor is a bit morbid."

"Indeed," she said. "How about we make this game interesting? You can only put down a word that pertains to our current situation. If you don't have any interesting letters, you can switch out some of your letters for new ones."

"Okay." Drake used one of the *G*s in *DRUGGED* and spelled G-A-M-E. "That's what this is, right? This is a game Janine is playing, some sort of comeuppance for past indiscretions?"

"Past indiscretions?" Talia seemed a bit unnerved. "Last time I checked, grand theft and potential murder are crimes punishable by jail or even death."

"*GAME* is fourteen points. The *M*, placed over a double word score space, gets me thirty-four total points," said Drake.

Talia switched out a few of her letters from the pile in the middle of the table. She used the *E* in *GAME* to end the word *FREE*.

"*Free.* The truth will set you free. That was the promise, or threat, from Janine. A double letter score for *F* gives me eleven points. That is twenty-eight total points for me so far," said Talia.

"Clever," admitted Drake.

Drake used the *R* in *RIPTIDE* to spell R-A-P-E. "That's why you are here, right Talia? You claimed you were raped by the general manager at your last hotel in New York. Isn't that right?"

"I am not going to talk about that," Talia said adamantly. "Especially not to you. It was a horribly traumatic event, and I won't speak of it."

"Okay, the *E* covered a double word space, so that makes twelve points. I now have forty-six points. Looks like I am way ahead," gloated Drake.

"Don't be so sure." Talia placed the word *POISON* on the board, using the *P* in *RIPTIDE*. "Poison. That was how Mrs. Matheson died, wasn't it? Or was it the fall from the balcony? What I hear from the interns was that you were the last person to see her alive. Is that correct?"

"Touché," Drake stated, looking slightly impressed by Talia's gall to say such a thing. He slammed the table with his right hand, and the loose Scrabble tiles bounced around. "I am not going to talk about that. I think we are done playing this game."

Chapter Twenty-Four

Janine

Gracie came back to the Opulence Resort and Spa the Wednesday before spring break. She dropped by the executive office and asked me if I would like to go out for cocktails after work to discuss something important. She said her idea was bold and exciting, and I could not wait to find out what adventure she had in store for us.

After two frozen margaritas in the lobby bar, Gracie blurted out, "I think Drake, the assistant general manager, had something to do with my mother's death."

"What? Oh my God . . . holy shit! . . . and what makes you say that?" I was utterly shocked.

Gracie said, "I overheard my dad talking to those two cops a few weeks ago. You know, that fat one and the skinny one. They are here pretty often, haven't you noticed? Well, they told my dad that Drake was the last person to see my mom alive, then something about a delayed toxicology report and poison, and then something about fainting or falling off the balcony."

"What are you saying, Gracie? You think Drake poisoned and then killed your mom? Why would he do that?"

Suddenly emboldened, Gracie stood up and said, "You and I, along with those two bozo cops, are going to devise a plan to get Drake to confess. We have a lot of work to do and less than ten days to do it before I have to get back to school. Let's go. My mom needs us to find out the truth."

Chapter Twenty-Five

The Executive Suite

Drake got up from the dining room table and walked toward his jacket, which was hanging on one of the kitchen barstools. He sifted through one of his pockets and pulled out six Hershey's Kisses.

"Aah," said Talia. "You scared me there for a bit. I didn't know what you were about to pull out. You must still have Jason's knife in your pants pocket. I was wondering what other lethal weapons you may have in your possession."

"So, what, now you are afraid of me or what I might do?"

"Hardly," said Talia. "I can take care of myself. I am not afraid of anyone, and I know how to protect myself against predators."

"Hmm, well, here. I have a few kisses for you." Drake handed Talia three of his candies, then winked at her.

"Thank you, I think I will watch you eat your chocolates first, and to be clear, these are the only kisses I will accept from you."

"Relax, I am not a rapist," he assured her.

"What are you then?" asked Talia.

"What am *I?*" asked Drake. "What are *you?*" Off they went again.

The grandfather clock clanged five times. Evening had arrived. Five o'clock this Saturday evening at the Opulence meant that the ToyCon gala dinner had just begun, and the banquet staff was preparing for the Winston wedding, which would commence beachside at sunset, a few short hours from now.

The whistle blew, this time for three full seconds, and Drake and Talia covered their ears, hoping to protect their precious eardrums from the pain. Two of the floorboards in the living room lit up in florescent-green neon the color of a glow stick.

"There, Drake. Look at the floor. I guess you forgot to check the floorboards when you were searching the walls and cabinets for an escape," said Talia.

Drake ignored what was becoming an annoying commentary, removed Jason's knife from his pocket, and used the blade to lift up the boards. Underneath lay a single sheet of paper.

"It's a resume," said Drake. "It is your resume, Talia. This is getting very interesting now," he said, baiting her.

"Give me that," demanded Talia.

"Nope," said Drake as he lifted it above his head so Talia could not reach it.

"You are a child," said Talia, exasperated.

Chapter Twenty-Six

Janine

We devised a plan that we thought was foolproof. According to Merriam-Webster, *foolproof* means "a plan so simple, plain, or reliable as to leave no opportunity for error, misuse, or failure." Boy, were we wrong about that.

Chapter Twenty-Seven

The Executive Suite

D rake took great interest in Talia's resume. After a minute or so of glancing over it, he said, "Well, my my, how interesting. You went from being a banquet waiter to a catering manager, then after just one year, you were promoted to director of food and beverage. That is quite an accomplishment. I have never heard of anyone going from catering sales to director of F&B in only a years' time."

"When I was working in New York, I booked over thirty weddings that year and took in almost $2.5 million," Talia said proudly.

"I think there is more to that story. In fact, I am sure of it," suggested Drake.

"Really? Tell me about what you think you know, Drake."

"I heard that you claimed you were raped by the general manager at the New York Towers Hotel in Manhattan."

"Okay, then what?" asked Talia. "You seem to know so much. Tell me the whole story you claim to know."

"My understanding is that you filed a report with human resources stating that you were raped by Mr. Lewis, the general manager."

"Go on," said Talia.

"Well, I heard that he denied that he ever touched you and that he claimed you came on to him. Shortly after, he was transferred to Hawaii, which is hardly a place one would get transferred to if the story were true, and you got promoted to director of food and beverage here at the Opulence Resort just to keep your mouth shut."

"Really."

"From what I heard, you lied in order to get promoted."

"And who did you hear that from?" asked Talia.

"All the guys at last month's executive management meeting."

"Exactly! Key words: 'all the guys'! Of course you heard the story that way. Do you believe them?"

"Yeah, after spending some time here with you. Yeah, I think I do believe that

you could have made up that story.
Otherwise, why would you be here in
this suite?"

Chapter Twenty-Eight

Janine

Gracie convinced the detectives to work with the two of us. The plan was to get Drake to admit what happened the night of Mrs. Matheson's death.

Gracie suggested we trap Drake in the executive suite and keep him there until he confessed.

The detectives suggested we lure him there under the pretense of a meeting, after making sure all of the rooms were fitted for sound and surveillance.

I agreed to send out the invitation and that I would also invite a few other managers so that the meeting would not seem suspicious.

The detectives were worried that it would be too risky to get others involved because something could go wrong or someone could get hurt.

Then I sold my pitch: "What if I told you that you could potentially make more than one arrest?"

"More than one?" asked Bobby, the young, skinny detective.

"This is not a good idea," said Stan, the portly one.

"Well, what if I told you that I am privy to certain information about particular hotel executives who are guilty of crimes, such as felony theft and potentially murder?" I said, trying to slightly suppress my intense enthusiasm. "Gracie and I have devised a way to get these executive managers into the suite and force them to admit their indiscretions. Then you two can arrest them."

"That sounds oversimplified," said Stan. "Nothing like that could happen so easily or go off without a hitch."

I handed the detectives a ten-page plan for how to get the suspected perpetrators to admit their guilt. It was written like a screenplay, except that it had contingency plans for different scenarios that could potentially occur.

Working in the hotel business, you become extremely proficient with worst-case scenarios. For example, what if there is a storm? What room would you move the wedding to? What if the flowers, the cake, or the photographer do not arrive in time or at all? Do you have a backup florist, baker, and photographer that could accommodate a party of two hundred fifty people in a pinch?

Gracie suggested exactly how she would set the room in the finest detail for the sting operation. "I think we should call it 'Operation Opulence,'" she said proudly. I thought that was funny, but no one laughed except Gracie and me.

Detective Bobby looked dumbfounded.

Stan chimed in. "I am going to have to speak with the sergeant about this to get approval, but I am very interested. Very interested."

Chapter Twenty-Nine

The Executive Suite

The grandfather clock chimed seven times. Talia said, "The melody . . . the melody that played before the chimes, it changed."

"What do you mean?" asked Drake.

"Well, usually on the hour, the clock plays a melody and then chimes. The usual melody is 'Ave Maria,' but this time it was something else, something familiar." Talia took a few moments to think about it, then said, "I know. The clock melody was 'Jingle Bells.'" Talia's eyes flashed with anger.

"Very funny, Janine," shouted Talia, yelling up toward the speaker in the ceiling.

"What is so funny about 'Jingle Bells'?" asked Drake. He was surely amused at this point.

"I was nearly raped on Christmas Eve last year," Talia said angrily.

"Nearly?" asked Drake.

"I thought you said you were raped, not nearly raped."

"I am pretty sure I didn't say anything at all to you, Drake."

"So you mean allegedly, almost raped," said Drake.

"You are an ass," said Talia angrily.

The familiar sound of the gut-wrenching whistle filled the room once again.

"Goddamn it, Janine, enough with the whistle. It's obnoxious," said Talia.

Just then, a toy train marked "The Polar Express" chugged through the living room, flashing red lights and tooting its tiny air whistle. For additional effect, green smoke was emitted through the locomotive chimney, rather robustly. Each train car was filled with miniature candy canes. Drake started laughing—a real, belly-busting laugh.

"This is not funny," said Talia. But then Talia gave in to a bit of laughter.

They chuckled and enjoyed a few moments of glee before Drake said, "Well, you said Janine was all about theatrics."

"I did say that, didn't I?"

"How in the hell did she wangle this one?" asked Drake, really enjoying this moment.

"I think the train came from under the credenza. It must have been there all along, probably engineered to turn on by remote. That is just pure genius. Remind me to hire Janine for my high-end themed catering events. Her ideas are limitless," mused Talia.

"Candy canes—that is one way to freshen our breath. I haven't brushed my teeth since Friday morning. How about you?"

"None of your business, but since you asked, I carry a toothbrush and toothpaste in my purse, along with makeup and deodorant for that matter. I work twelve-to-fifteen-hour days. I always have to be fresh and ready to greet staff and clients, and it works a whole lot better than Hershey's Kisses," Talia added sarcastically.

Chapter Thirty

Janine

F riday morning, Gracie, the two
detectives—Bobby and Stan—
and I set up the executive suite
for "Operation Opulence." The Palm
Beach Police had no official name for
this sting, but it made Gracie happy to
give it an alias or stage name.

Unfortunately, the sergeant did not
agree to all of the plans we suggested
because he was concerned that a few of
our ideas were dangerous or had too big
of a risk of going awry. Gracie and I also
had to agree to certain stipulations to
move forward. For example, we could
not tell Mr. Matheson about the plan,
which made no sense to me at the time,
and we had to block off the rose garden
and courtyard by the wishing well so no
guests could happen by, along with a
few other conditions that I was not
thrilled about, but their goal was safety
first. That was to be expected when you
partner with the police, so we complied.

After three full dress rehearsals, as they call it in the theatre business, we were ready to "break a leg." Just a bit of theatre humor to set the mood.

As planned, at exactly 4:45 p.m., I sent out an urgent meeting invite to all involved for 7:00 p.m. in the executive suite. And so, the game began.

Chapter Thirty-One

The Executive Suite

The grandfather clock chimed eight times, then an hour later, nine. Each time, the "Jingle Bells" melody preceded the clanging bell chimes.

"Okay, Drake, it's your turn," said Talia. "It's been two hours since we heard from Janine, and I am hot, hungry, dehydrated, and exhausted. I am tired of being watched like a lab experiment. We need to get out of this rattrap. So spill the beans and let's go."

"Oh, I'm sorry, I thought we were still on *your* turn. I don't remember you mentioning that you lied about the alleged attempted rape," said Drake. "You have to admit your crime before you can leave. It's been two hours since the Polar Express Christmas spectacle, and I don't think Santa rewards bad little girls."

"Funny, Drake, but again, women don't lie about that kind of shit! IT IS YOUR TURN."

Silence, then a sound—a loud sound—but this time it was not a whistle. It was an ambulance siren followed by a fire engine bell.

"I am going to guess these were the sounds you heard the night Mrs. Matheson fell to her death, right Drake? And, just like that, it's your turn. This is going to be good."

The emergency lights in the room flickered, then turned off, and only the moonlight shining through the balcony's sliding glass doors kept them from total darkness.

The sconces on the balcony's terrace switched on, thunder clapped in the distance, and a figure of a woman stood on the terrace, draped in an elegant, white-lace gown that flowed vigorously in the wind due to the looming storm. She looks like an angel, thought Talia. "It's Janine. No, wait. It's Gracie."

"How did she get there?" asked Drake.

They both rushed to the sliding glass doors, which were now miraculously unlocked.

They opened the doors, and there stood Gracie. She drew a bottle of champagne out from behind her back.

"Would you like a glass, Drake?" Gracie asked eerily. "Are you worried it might be poisoned? Wouldn't you like to have a glass of the same champagne you used to poison and murder my mother?"

Chapter Thirty-Two

Janine

Watching the teammates' faces contort in horror the moment they all realized they were trapped was electrifying. We had such joy that we were able to pull this off.

Gracie's imagination and executive suite set design were brilliant. Stan and Bobby did an excellent job with the camera and microphone placement. They placed multiple bugs in places no one would think to look, like inside door hinges and electrical outlets. Translucent bugs were placed high above in chandeliers, and opaque bugs were concealed on the inner feet of the furniture. Tiny cameras were set up— not on the ceiling where they would be expected but rather at eye level so that every sound came across crisply and clearly. The cameras were easily hidden in the walls of every room, nestled in between the three-inch-thick, wave-textured wall panels that resembled cascading ocean waves or the wood-paneled walls in the office and bedrooms.

Piece by piece, we sent evidence into the suite that would unveil secrets and expose atrocities, which was long overdue.

With every little detail, our plan was followed and executed swimmingly—until it wasn't.

Chapter Thirty-Three

The Executive Suite

Drake was shocked into silence by Gracie's accusations. He took what seemed like an eternity to gather the right words to say and the composure to convey them.

"Gracie, I blame myself every day for your mother's death. I am truly sorry for your loss and my own, but the circumstances that surrounded her untimely demise are misunderstood by everyone except me. Please come inside so we can talk about this."

"No!" shouted Gracie. "You cannot smooth-talk your way out of this! Just tell me what happened."

"I want to tell you the whole story, but I need time to explain. Please come in off the balcony, and I'll tell you everything."

"No, I am staying right here," said Gracie adamantly.

"Okay then, I'll just show you." Drake reached into the right pocket of his shirt.

He pulled out a photo. "I keep this photo close to my heart. It means the world to me."

Talia grabbed the photo, looked at it —seeming shocked—then handed it to Gracie.

Gracie, shedding a single tear, asked, "What is this?"

"It is a photo of your mom and me with you. Did you ever wonder why I attended every birthday party, dance recital, and musical you performed in? I am much more than a family friend. I have worked with your dad for over twenty years, and your mom and I were friends; we were best friends. More than that, I loved her. When your mom was having difficulty getting pregnant, she came to me for help. She suspected early on that your dad was infertile, but she never had the guts to tell him. She feared he would get angry and hurt her. Telling a man like him that he could be infertile would be emasculating."

Gracie was visibly shaken by the news, sobbing now. "More than friends? You 'loved her'? He would have hurt her?"

"Yes, Gracie, he has a terrible temper. I am sure he did a great job at hiding it from you, but once you left for school, his temper flared worse than ever."

"I just can't believe that. That is not the man I know," cried Gracie.

"Gracie, people are not always what they seem. I am your father. Your mom and I agreed to keep it a secret, but your father figured it out shortly before your mom died."

"What? How? I don't understand."

"Mr. Matheson went to a fertility clinic last year without telling your mom. He wondered why she never got pregnant with another child after all these years. He wondered if maybe he could be the reason; maybe he was infertile. He was lonely once you left for college and desperately wanted another child. The clinic confirmed what he subconsciously already knew: that he was sterile. I was sitting with him in the office when that call came in. He was devastated, and I knew he suspected that I was your father. I believe it was he who poisoned the champagne. The poison was intended for both of us. Your dad wanted to kill us both, but only your mom drank the champagne. I didn't."

Gracie was sobbing uncontrollably, and Drake reached forward to hug her.

Gracie stepped back—one, two, three steps—then tumbled off the balcony.

Chapter Thirty-Four

Janine
The Plan

There is a pivotal moment in the musical *Mean Girls* where, once Regina gets her revenge, she says, "Sometimes what's meant to break you makes you brave." These words brought comfort to me as the finale unfolded.

In the final act, Gracie appeared on the balcony, illuminated by moonlight in her beautiful, white gown as the thunderstorm raged in the distance. Selfishly, I was thinking, This is the perfect backdrop to the climax of our play. I could not imagine anything could go wrong.

We anticipated that Drake would admit to poisoning Gracie's mother. We were not prepared for Drake to accuse Mr. Matheson of her murder.

The plan was to accuse Drake of poisoning Mrs. Matheson. He, of course, would initially deny it. Gracie would provoke him and then push him, hoping he would, in turn, push her. She would seemingly fall off the balcony to her death. At that point, Drake would see what he had done, now responsible for two women falling off the balcony, and admit what he did to Mrs. Matheson. Stan and Bobby would then open the executive suite doors and arrest him.

Gracie, attached by cables, was supposed to fall, then get pulled into the suite below by Bobby, just like flying in her *Peter Pan* play at school. Stan would throw a life-sized dummy out of the window, which they practiced many times. The dummy would fall into the wishing well. The dummy was essential for unassuming bystanders to witness, creating credibility and provoking the 911 call. Janine would already be lying by the well, bloodied, wearing the same gown, face concealed by her hair, and ready for Stan and Bobby to get called to the scene to haul the body away.

The balcony fall and subsequent pretend death of Gracie was a bit over-the-top for me, and the police sergeant felt it was very risky as well, but Gracie insisted. Gracie was very particular about the theatrics of it all. For her, it was not just about exposing criminals. She wanted her mom's killer to be exposed in grandiose style. For her, the fall was nonnegotiable. She called it her "fall from grace."

Talia was our ace in the hole. She was invited into the suite at the suggestion of Stan and Bobby. She was already being accused of lying about an alleged rape last year, so it made sense to invite her into our plan. She had to make everything move smoothly in the suite, keep the teammates away from areas we needed access to, and most importantly, push Drake away from the balcony once Gracie fell over so he wouldn't see the ground until Janine was ready and in position. Talia had to distract Drake for what we calculated was three minutes. That would be enough time to pull Gracie into the suite below and throw out the dummy body double.

The idea was that, once Drake saw the body on the ground, he would break.

Chapter Thirty-Five

The Executive Suite

Gracie fell off the balcony, and Talia pushed Drake away from the bannister. Gracie was pulled into the suite below by Bobby, and Stan threw the dummy out the window. In spite of the wind provoked by the looming storm, the dummy fell directly into the well. Janine was bloodied and in place, playing dead.

"Drake, no! Don't look down there!" screamed Talia. Talia held him back as long as she physically could. Drake could not help himself, and after a few minutes or so, he had to see for himself.

Upon seeing the body on the pavement in the rose garden below, Drake started to unravel. He was pacing about, crying out to God, asking "Why, God, why?" and crying inconsolably. He took Jason's knife out of his pants pocket.

"No, no, no, no, Drake, please! This is not your fault! This is not what it seems —please, no!"

Drake stabbed himself in the stomach just as Stan and Bobby rushed through the doors of the executive suite.

"Call for an ambulance," said Stan. Then they both rushed down the hidden passage to the elevator and out to the garden to attend to Janine once the 911 call came through about a jumper at the Opulence.

Carried away on stretchers followed by staff and prying hotel guests, Janine and Drake were placed in separate ambulances and whisked away. Janine met up with Gracie, Bobby, and Stan later by Drake's bedside at the Palm Beach Hospital.

"Gracie, you are alive!" Drake said, elated, once he opened his eyes after a two-hour abdominal surgery. I saw you fall and then, well, how could you have survived?"

"I am so sorry," said Gracie sincerely. "I had no idea about you and Mom, and I freaked out. Please forgive me. I'm sorry I made you believe that—"

"It's okay," Drake interrupted. "It's okay." Both Drake and Gracie were crying now. "We have each other," Drake said. "We are going to be just fine. It's what your mom would want for us."

"Forgive me, Dad. I promise we will work through this."

Suddenly noticing that Bobby, Stan, and Janine were also in the room, Drake locked eyes with the three of them. One by one, he sternly pointed a finger at each of them and said, "You all have a lot of explaining to do."

"YES, SIR!" said Stan. "You just concentrate on getting some sleep and feeling better. We will explain everything in the morning."

Epilogue

E ven though it has been a year since the incident in the executive suite, it feels like it just happened yesterday. Gracie and I knew the one-year mark was the perfect time to revisit the Opulence Resort.

I threw a penny into the wishing well and made a wish. It was more of a thanks really, gratitude that I met Gracie. She has become such a great friend. Then Gracie threw her penny into the well. She said, "We did it for you, Mom. I wish for you to find peace."

We walked over to the beach and sat on the sand. There is nothing quite like a sunset in South Florida. It is truly breathtaking. The awe and wonder of its grace just makes your worries seem so small.

"It still angers me that Jason was released from jail twenty-four hours after being detained," I said.

"Me too."

"Bobby said that the star witness, Alicia—who witnessed the death of Mr.

Jones at the Miami Airport Hotel—had been reported missing. No witness, no proof of the crime. I'll bet Jason had something to do with her disappearance," I suggested.

"I guess we will never know," said Gracie. "It is a shame that the hotel did not file charges against Adam for theft, but at least they made him repay what he stole. Surely he had to sell his coveted stocks," she mused.

Gracie and I made a pact that our detective days were over.

"I really am truly sorry about the pain we inflicted upon Drake," I said. "I never would have guessed that he and your mom . . . well, I am happy you two are working things out and getting along well. When will Mr. Matheson be released from prison?"

"No idea, and I don't care, but I believe since he confessed to both murder and attempted murder and there will not be a trial, he will serve twenty-five years."

The waves crashed into the sand, and it felt as though each and every wave washed away a bit of the pain we had endured over the past year.

Talia came up from behind us and kicked sand in our hair. "What are you two bitches doing here?" said Talia with her usual lighthearted sarcastic demeanor.

"Hey, Talia, congratulations on your promotion to general manager. You deserve it," I said.

"Definitely," said Gracie.

"What are you two up to? No good, I am sure," said Talia mischievously.

"I am working at the Sand Dunes Resort, and Gracie is finishing college. We are currently working on a screenplay titled *Murder at the Opulence Hotel.* Look for it at the Cannes film festival someday soon!"

Turn the page for a short
Halloween story.

The Old Lady in the Gazebo

Sarah used to walk home from work in the evenings from a restaurant in Fort Lauderdale where she worked as a waitress. The walk home took her past the park and over the train tracks. On her way home, she noticed an old lady and her cat sitting in the gazebo in the park. Each night, the lady would wave to her as she passed by on her way home. Sarah thought, The next time I work, I will bring the old lady some leftover food. She seems so nice, and I am sure she must be lonely and hungry out there all alone.

The following evening, Sarah brought the old lady half of her turkey sandwich that she could not finish on her dinner break. The old lady was very thankful. She smiled and took Sarah's hand into her own and said, "Watch out."

Sarah was taken a bit off guard with that sentiment but assumed that the lady was just old and maybe a bit senile. She could also be worried about me walking home alone at night in the early morning hours, she thought. Sarah smiled and said, "Okay, have a nice night."

121

The next time Sarah worked, she brought the old lady a portion of her pasta that she could not finish during her dinner break. The old lady was again very thankful. She smiled and uttered the word "for."

Sarah said, "Enjoy the meal. See you next time."

A few nights later, Sarah brought the old woman half of her hamburger with french fries. The old woman was very thankful. This time Sarah expected the woman to tell her another cryptic word or words. So she waited patiently for the woman to speak. The old woman looked directly into her eyes with a cold stare and said the words "the sun." Sarah said, "Hmmm, 'watch out for the sun'? What does that mean?" The old lady just smiled and said nothing else. Sarah thought, Okay, Florida is very sunny, and sometimes the UV rays can get to dangerous levels, but it is October. The sun is not so hot in October. The lady is probably just worried about me. She just wants me to take care of myself. Maybe I'll buy makeup with sunscreen, she thought—just to be safe. "She is so nice," Sarah said out loud to herself while continuing her walk home.

Halloween evening, Sarah worked until the wee hours of the morning. The restaurant was very busy with college students parading around in their costumes and drinking until the restaurant manager literally pushed out the remaining patrons because the doors had to close by 2:00 a.m.

Sarah was exhausted and famished after working such long hours. She ordered a large piece of carrot cake that the chef made specially for Halloween. It was delicious, but Sarah could only finish half of it. She packed up the other half for the old woman to enjoy. On the way home, however, Sarah decided not to give the old woman the other half of her carrot cake. This evening, when she passed the park, she told the old woman she did not have anything for her to eat tonight. The carrot cake was so good she wanted to keep it for herself and enjoy it the following day. She apologized to the old woman and continued on her way.

Sarah crossed over the train tracks and was hit head-on by the Sun Train. The old woman was standing beside her once the train passed. She looked down upon her broken, mangled body and uttered the word . . . "train."

Special Thanks

I wish to thank my editor, Anna Roberts, for her editing expertise and finesse. I would like to thank my mother for her hypercritical thinking skills and countless games of Scrabble I have yet to win. A special thanks to my daughters, the "twisted sisters," for their alleged love of everything I write, before even opening the attachment to read. I would also like to thank my husband for his encouragement and The Great Escape Room in Jacksonville, which my brilliant family members and I could not escape. That unsuccessful adventure inspired me to write this story.

About the Author

Leah Orr worked in hospitality management. Leah has written four children's books. She lives in Jensen Beach, Florida, with her husband and three children. *The Executive Suite* is her debut novella.